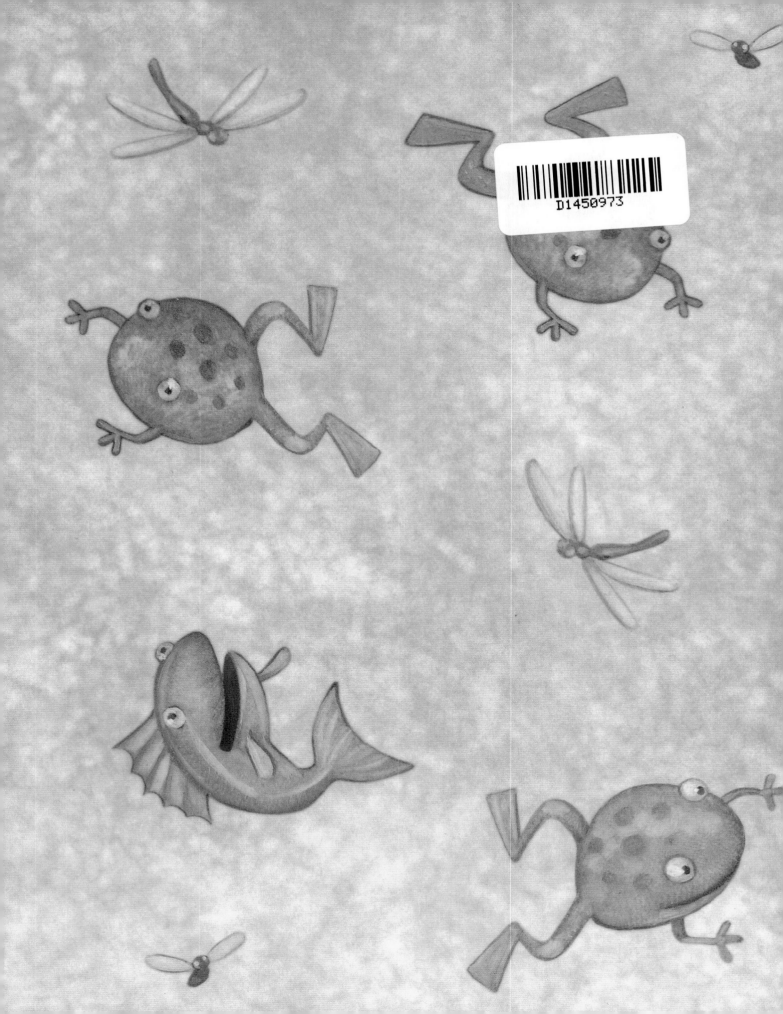

D1450973

Let's Have a
Daddy
Day

KAREN *NEW YORK TIMES*
BESTSELLING AUTHOR
KINGSBURY

ILLUSTRATED BY
DAN ANDREASEN

ZONDERkidz

ZONDERVAN.com/
AUTHORTRACKER
follow your favorite authors

To Donald, my forever love
Kelsey, my bright sunshine
Tyler, my favorite song
Sean, my smiley boy
Josh, my gentle giant
EJ, my chosen one
Austin, my miracle child
And to God Almighty, who has—for now—blessed me with these.

—K.K.

For Katrina

—D.A.

ZONDERKIDZ

Let's Have a Daddy Day
Copyright © 2010 by Karen Kingsbury
Illustrations © 2010 by Dan Andreasen

Requests for information should be addressed to:
Zondervan, *Grand Rapids, Michigan 49530*

Library of Congress Cataloging-in-Publication Data

Kingsbury, Karen.
    Let's Have a Daddy Day / by Karen Kingsbury; illustrations by Dan Andreasen.
        p. cm.
    Summary: A father describes several possibilities for sharing special time with his children, but finally realizes that just playing and laughing together are fun and will be remembered warmly.
    ISBN 978-0-310-71215-2 (jacketed hardcover)
    1. Father and child—Fiction. 2. Stories in rhyme. I. Andreasen, Dan, ill. II Title. III. Title: Let's Have a Daddy Day.
PZ8.3.K6145Ld 2008
[E]—dc22   2007023109

All Scripture quotations, unless otherwise indicated, are taken from the *Holy Bible, New International Version®. NIV®.* Copyright © 1973, 1978, 1984 by International Bible Society. Used by permission of Zondervan. All rights reserved..

Any Internet addresses (websites, blogs, etc.) and telephone numbers printed in this book are offered as a resource. They are not intended in any way to be or imply an endorsement by Zondervan, nor does Zondervan vouch for the content of these sites and numbers for the life of this book.

All rights reserved. No part of this publication may be reproduced, stored in a retrieval system, or transmitted in any form or by any means—electronic, mechanical, photocopy, recording, or any other—except for brief quotations in printed reviews, without the prior permission of the publisher.

Published in association with the literary agency of Alive Communication, Inc.
7680 Goddard Street #200, Colorado Springs, CO 80920.
www.alivecommunications.com

Zonderkidz is a trademark of Zondervan.

Editor: Betsy Flikkema
Design: Laura Maitner-Mason

Printed in China

10 11 12 13 • 5 4 3 2 1

Let's go on a Daddy Day, a time for me and you.
Today while you're still little, there're so many things to do!

A Daddy Day would be a blast; what fun this day could be.
Side by side we'll build a fort in that old backyard tree.

We'll need some sturdy plywood and a hammer and some nails,
elbow grease and sawdust, and our lunch inside a pail.

But if the rain from yesterday has made the tree too wet,
we'll build that house another day. It can't be done just yet!

So how about some tadpoles? Canby Creek has lots of those.
Then we would have a Daddy Day with squishy, soggy toes.

Those squirmy, squiggly, tadpoles—we'll chase 'em, and we'll catch 'em.
Maybe find an egg or two; we'll take 'em home and hatch 'em.

And if we watch them patiently, we'll see them sprout webbed feet.
And someday soon they'll jump the pail—now won't that be a treat?

And if, when we get to the creek, the tadpoles are all frogs—
sitting, jumping, snatching flies from high atop the logs—
we'll just go to another place where we can have some fun
and play together side by side—we'll laugh and jump and run.

The lake would be the perfect spot to play as army rangers
looking out for bad guys as we dodge around the dangers.
Three or four masked bandits and a hooligan or two—
our trail will be a treacherous one, but we'll know what to do!

And if the day is so hot that the lake becomes jam-packed,
we'll go and get your bat and glove, your ball and baseball cap.

We'll ride out to the vacant lot and play a baseball game.
With nerves of steel I'll pitch to you as fans scream out your name!

The crowd it roars, the runner scores, the game's tied two to two.
And in the ninth the slugger's up—the MVP—that's you!

And when your hit sails way beyond the farthest outfield stands,
you'll round the bases, tip your hat to all the screaming fans.

But if we find a building standing on that vacant lot,
we'll choose another game to play and find a different spot.

So what about our Daddy Day? You're growing way too fast.
We need a wild adventure now before this day has passed.

We don't need bats or cowboy hats to have some fun together.
Don't need saddles, nails, or jars, or perfect shady weather.

'Cause hey, we're here! We're side by side! Let's drop down to the floor.
Let's wrestle till we laugh and cry and shout out loud, "No more!"

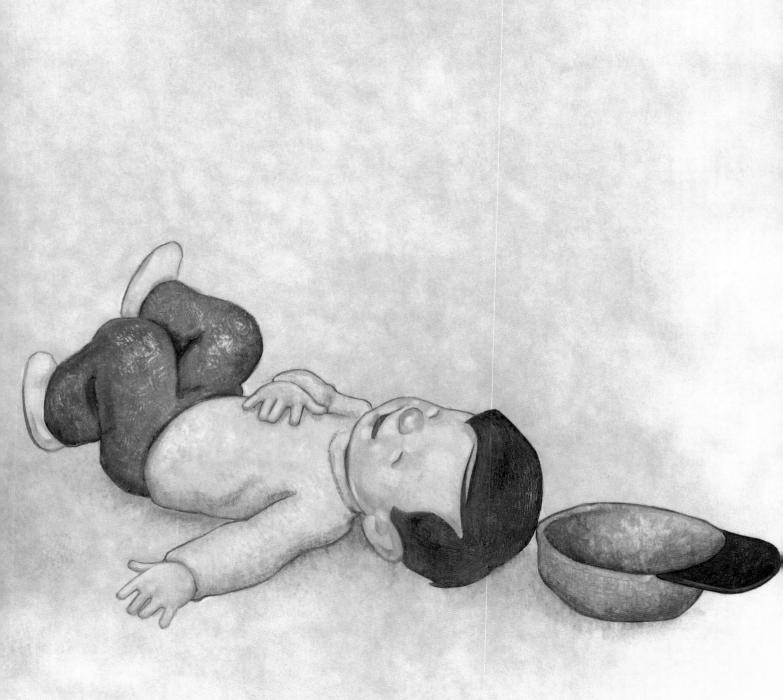

So when you're all grown up and you look back upon this day,
you'll know how much I loved you 'cause we took the time to play.

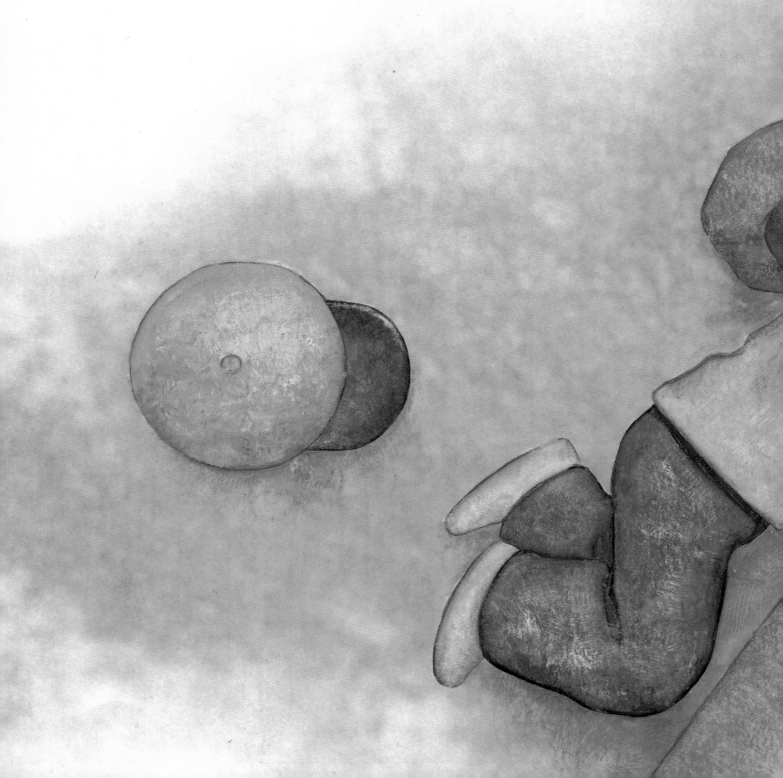

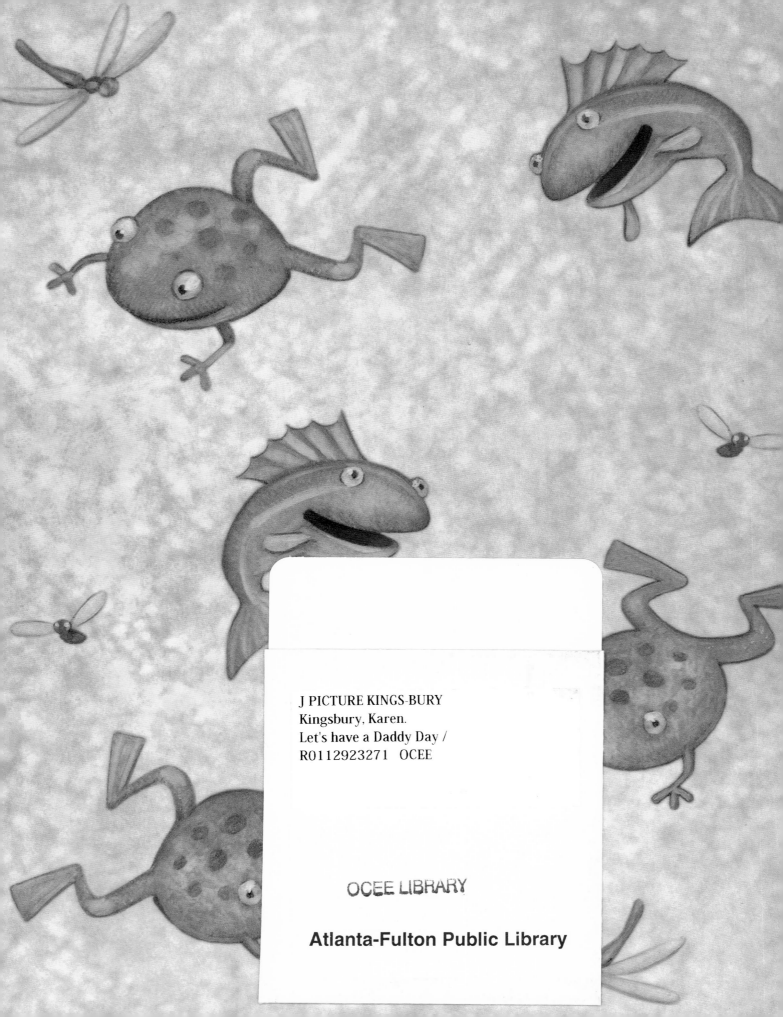

J PICTURE KINGS-BURY
Kingsbury, Karen.
Let's have a Daddy Day /
R0112923271   OCEE

OCEE LIBRARY

Atlanta-Fulton Public Library